to Jennifer

enjoy my book!

Bianca Davis

THE ATLANTIC SALMON

◆◆◆◆◆◆◆

TEXT AND PHOTOGRAPHS BY **BIANCA LAVIES**

DUTTON CHILDREN'S BOOKS
NEW YORK

Acknowledgments
For sharing time, knowledge, and thoughts, thanks
to Alfred L. Meister, formerly chief biologist of
the Atlantic Salmon Commission, State of Maine; and
to Rick Jordan, Maine Department of Inland Fisheries
and Wildlife, formerly of the Maine Atlantic Sea-Run
Salmon Commission.

The publisher wishes to thank Jonothan Logan for his
contribution to this project.

Copyright © 1992 by Bianca Lavies

All rights reserved.

Library of Congress Cataloging-in-Publication Data

Lavies, Bianca.
   The Atlantic salmon/by Bianca Lavies.—1st ed.
     p.   cm.
   Summary: Text and photographs depict the life cycle of the
Atlantic salmon, from its birth in freshwater streams through its
journey to the sea to its return to spawn in its streams of origin.
   ISBN 0-525-44860-8
   1. Atlantic salmon—Juvenile literature.   2. Atlantic salmon—
Life cycles—Juvenile literature.   [1. Atlantic salmon.   2. Salmon.]
I. Title.
QL638.S2L38   1992
597'.55—dc20   91-27990   CIP   AC

Published in the United States by Dutton Children's Books,
a division of Penguin Books USA Inc.
375 Hudson Street, New York, New York 10014

Designer: Joseph Rutt

Printed in Hong Kong by South China Printing Co.
First Edition   10 9 8 7 6 5 4 3 2 1

To my cat, Ginger, who loves salmon too.

In the chilly days of late fall, the creatures of this clear, fast-rushing stream in Maine prepare for winter. Fish lay eggs that will hatch in the spring. Mink, otters, and muskrats hunt for freshwater food—mussels and crayfish—to build up their fat reserves.

Most of these animals spend their whole lives in the tumbling stream, never venturing farther than a few days' travel from here. But one creature among them, the Atlantic salmon, is destined to lead a more far-ranging life. Here it is born, and here its days may end; yet the stream is not its only home.

A great deal has been happening inside this salmon egg since it was deposited and fertilized in the gravel streambed last fall. Now, at the end of April, changes that have been occurring all spring are visible. Where once there was only orange fluid, the outlines of a tiny salmon embryo can be seen. The embryo's large, dark eyes became distinct early on; other organs and structures took shape as the winter weeks passed. The yellow-orange yolk supplies all the energy and material the growing embryo needs.

When the embryo becomes fully developed, it uses its tail to wriggle and twist free. The egg's once-strong outer membrane is now fragile and easily broken. Not yet able to find food for itself, the newly hatched salmon remains attached to its yolk sac for nourishment. At this early stage, the salmon is called an *alevin* (pronounced AL-e-vin).

In both photos you can just make out the fine bones of the alevin's spine. Fish are an ancient line of animals, the first vertebrates—animals with backbones—to have appeared on earth.

Under six to twelve inches of sheltering stones, hundreds of tiny alevins share a gravel nest. For this photograph, a little gravel has been pushed aside to let us look inside the *redd*, as salmon nests are often called. Dug by the mother salmon when she laid her eggs in the fall, the nest offers protection from the many animals—birds,

salamanders, large insects, and other fish—that would prey on the salmon eggs and small hatchlings. The nest also offers protection against sudden rises in water level, caused by melting snow or spring rains, that otherwise might dislodge the eggs.

Within a few weeks, the inch-long salmon use up their yolk sacs and begin to look more like fish. *Fry,* as they are called at this stage, must now leave the redd to find food for themselves. At night, under the cover of darkness, they wriggle their way up through the gravel and seek a place safe from predators. At this time of year, late spring, there is usually plenty of food to be had, in the form of crustaceans, insect larvae, and other small organisms. The rapidly growing fry feed often, watching warily for danger with their large, side-looking eyes.

Fish need oxygen to live, no less than we humans do. They get it from the stream water, which traps air as it churns and tumbles along. The stream also contains oxygen given off by the green plants living there. When the salmon open their mouths, water enters and then passes out over gills at the sides of their heads. The gills extract the needed oxygen.

The free-flowing world above the nest is full of new opportunities and surprises—some of which are lethal. Here, a salmon fry scouting for food along the stony bottom finds sudden death when a dragonfly nymph snatches it for a meal. Mammals, amphibians, birds such as kingfishers and mergansers, and larger fish also eat salmon fry.

The returning salmon are magnificent silvery creatures with blue-black backs, full of energy stored during their years of feeding at sea. Fishermen know that the muscle and fat the salmon have accumulated make the fish delicious; and they know that the salmon must pass upriver to return to their home streams. Commercial fishermen net salmon in the open sea (though the salmon we eat comes increasingly from pen-reared, not wild, stock). Sport fishermen wait with rod and reel for the return of the salmon each spring. The catch of both is now tightly regulated by many governments.

Those salmon that escape the fishermen must use every ounce of their strength to fight their way upstream, against the onrushing current. Sometimes the obstacles are great, forcing the fish back, until, with mighty twists of their powerful tails, the salmon leap upward, ascending rapids and tall waterfalls. Obstacles made by humans, like dams, present the greatest challenge. The Atlantic salmon's scientific name, *Salmo salar,* derives from the Latin name the Romans gave it two thousand years ago, meaning "leaper."

Some three months after hatching, the salmon, now two to three inches long, reach the *parr* stage. Their distinctive pattern of dark bands, called parr marks, helps the fish blend into their surroundings.

Each parr claims a territory for itself, which it defends. Any small fish coming near—even a brother or sister—is warned off with a gesture of fins, followed by a nip if the intruder does not go away.

Although parr have many predators in the stream, the parr do not need to hide from predatory insects as they did when they were fry. In fact, in the photograph at right, a parr is having a dragonfly nymph

for dinner. Among the many insects parr eat are damselfly nymphs (shown at left, top two) and mayfly nymphs (bottom two). On occasion, salmon parr jump right out of the water to catch insects in the air, though it is more common for parr to snap them up at the water's surface.

A parr's life in the stream depends on excellent water quality, nearly pollution-free. Many rivers have lost their salmon population because of pollution by humans. In the United States, there are now regulations designed to prevent further losses.

Salmon parr usually live in the stream for several years, growing to a length of four to eight inches. Then, often toward the end of their third spring, the time arrives for each salmon to begin a great journey. Responding to water temperature and to other signals less well understood, the salmon drift downstream and make their way to the sea.

By the time a salmon begins its seaward migration, its parr marks have been obscured by a protective silvery coating. Other changes have also begun that will help it adapt to salt water.

Carried along by swift currents, the young *smolts*, as salmon are called when they turn silver and start their journey, pass from streams into rivers. They swim around boulders and over shallow rapids, feeding hungrily as they go. In North America, salmon from the New England states and Canada make such journeys. Finally they reach broad rivers that empty into the vast Atlantic Ocean.

Ocean water, dense with salt and other dissolved minerals, is very different from the fresh stream water the salmon have known. Most of the world's fish cannot make the great adjustment from fresh water to salt water, no matter how gradual the transition. Salmon, however, can. Special pumping cells in their gills, responsible for maintaining the balance of minerals in their bodies, enable them to adjust to the requirements of saltwater life.

This adjustment does take time—if the smolts move too rapidly from the river to the ocean, they may become temporarily immobilized. So, depending on temperature and other conditions, they spend a day or more drifting with the tides in the place where the river waters mix with the sea—the estuary. In estuaries along the northeast coast of North America, salmon make this transition. The estuary shown here is in Canada.

From the estuaries, the salmon make their way east and north, then strike out into the vast North Atlantic Ocean. They head for the icy waters off Labrador and Greenland, more than a thousand miles away. To these rich feeding grounds come Atlantic salmon not only from North America but from the United Kingdom, Ireland, Norway, Sweden, and other European countries as well.

The salmon travel mostly alone. Although their routes are known, how they find their way to their feeding waters—what guides them—is still largely a mystery. We do know that the salmon find abundant food in the northern seas, for they grow remarkably. Within a few years, eating fish, shrimp, and other marine organisms, they can reach nearly three feet and weigh upwards of eight pounds. Atlantic salmon as heavy as one hundred pounds have been reported caught by net fishermen.

Although Atlantic salmon thrive in the sea, they will not reproduce there. To continue their kind, the adults must somehow find their way back across the ocean to freshwater streams, usually the same streams where they were born. There, food and shelter and bubbling sweet water will nurture the growth of their eggs and young.

When the powerful urge to return comes over them, after one or more years in the ocean, the salmon set out for their home streams. They travel quickly, covering twenty-five to fifty miles a day for weeks on end. Experiments have shown that the fish use their memories of the varying smell and taste of water in different places to help find their way back, along with other signs and senses not well understood. The hormonal signals that set them off on their journey homeward are not fully documented, either.

Having cleared rapids and waterfalls, the salmon find a quiet pool in which to rest and gather strength. Bruises, cuts, and tears now scar the bodies of some, but they will gradually heal.

During the long run upstream the salmon do not eat. The hook on the male's jaw, which appears during its return from the sea, is not for catching food. It is part of the salmon's final preparations for spawning.

Traveling mostly at night, pausing by day to rest where the water is deep and the current less swift, the salmon press on. By now their skin coloration is dark and their flesh less red. Their fat reserves are being used for energy and to form fertile eggs and sperm.

By late fall and early winter, some returning salmon have been caught by fishermen or by other predators. Some have drifted downstream, injured and exhausted. But many have succeeded in reaching their home streams. There they pair off, and the female claims a stretch of streambed for nest building.

In this photo, the male stands guard while the female digs a saucerlike depression in the gravel with powerful thrusts of her tail. Some kinds of fish lay many thousands of eggs when they spawn, relying on quantity to compensate for the numbers that will be swept away or eaten owing to lack of protection or parental care. Salmon mothers lay about eight hundred eggs per pound of their weight, but they insure that their eggs have a good chance of survival by digging each redd as much as twelve inches deep in a well-chosen place.

When the nest is ready, the two parents hover over it. Both quiver with effort, gulping water, as the female releases her eggs and the male his fertilizing cloud of milt. Quickly, the female goes to work again, covering the eggs with gravel. Then she moves a little way upstream to prepare another redd for another round of egg laying and fertilizing—as many as eight times, in all, before she has completed spawning.

Now, at last, the salmon can rest. Some, perhaps ten to twenty percent, will die soon after spawning. Others will return immediately to the ocean to feed and rebuild their strength. Still others will remain in the stream over winter, and then return to sea. Unlike Pacific salmon, which always die immediately after spawning, Atlantic salmon can survive a second journey to sea. About ten percent will return to spawn a second time.

Some early peoples understood the life cycle of the Atlantic salmon in terms of mystery and magic. They believed that the fish that disappeared from the streams in spring died and somehow came back to life again later, full grown. They called salmon "the supernatural ones." Now we have gained a different view, though there is more still to be learned. We explain their long and perilous journeys by saying that salmon take advantage of the ocean's rich feeding grounds without giving up the nurturing shelter of the stream for their eggs and young.
    Those eggs and the tiny alevins that emerge from them each spring are the first fragile stages in the life cycle of mighty swimmers—the prized and majestic Atlantic salmon.

BIANCA LAVIES spent nearly two years traveling in Maine, New Brunswick, Quebec, Newfoundland, and Scotland, photographing Atlantic salmon.

In the picture above, she is lying on a bench of her own design, waiting for salmon to arrive and spawn in a stream in Maine. "To photograph the salmon, I built a three-foot-square transparent Plexiglas box, put it in the stream, and added three hundred and sixty pounds of diving weights to hold it in place," she says. "Then I placed the camera in the box. My plan was to lie on the bench with my head down in the box and look through the camera; but first I had to figure out how to make the bench adjustable to deal with changes in water level. Then I rigged fourteen strobes just above the water to light the scene. Test shots of a plastic salmon looked great. Now all I needed was real salmon to arrive.

"But then it began to rain—and rain and rain. It was the worst rainfall since 1870, and I was unable to get a single shot. I talked to several experts and discovered that Newfoundland salmon spawn later than Maine salmon. So I quickly loaded everything up and headed for Newfoundland, where I had better luck and got my spawning pictures."